Walt Disney's
Winnie the Pooh
AND
THE MISSING POTS

By Betty Birney
Illustrated by Russell Hicks

A GOLDEN BOOK • NEW YORK
Western Publishing Company, Inc., Racine, Wisconsin 53404

It was spring cleaning time in the Hundred-Acre Wood.

"I'm going to get rid of these beat-up old pots," said Kanga as she tidied up her kitchen. "I never use them anymore."

"What are you going to do with them, Mama?" asked Roo.

"I'll take them out to the Trash Tree when I'm finished here," Kanga answered.

"Why don't I bounce these over there for you, Kanga?" said Tigger.

"Me too!" shouted Roo.

Soon Tigger and Roo were bouncing through the Hundred-Acre Wood.

"Bet I can bounce twice as high as you can!" said Roo, giggling.

"Tiggers can bounce twice as high as anybody!" answered Tigger.

So Tigger and Roo began a bouncing contest, bouncing over rocks and fallen branches along the way.

When they reached the Trash Tree, Tigger and Roo were surprised to find that their pots had all disappeared.

Meanwhile, Winnie the Pooh opened his front door and said—to no one in particular—"Good morning, morning! Or should I say, good day, morning!"

Then something round and shiny caught his eye.

Pooh hurried to pick it up, thinking it might be a jar of honey. But instead, it was a battered tin pot.

"A present for me?" said Pooh. "And it's not even my birthday. I could use this to keep honey in!" Pooh scratched his head. "Now all I need is some honey."

Luckily, a bee came buzzing by, and Pooh followed it to a honey tree.

Rabbit was busy in his garden, hoeing furiously at a weed among his carrots, when suddenly his hoe hit something hard.

Rabbit bent over and picked up a battered tin pot.

"Did I grow this?" he wondered.

Then he had a bright idea.

"This is just what I've been looking for," he said, filling the pot with dirt and transplanting one of his prized carrots. "Now I can keep my favorite carrot plant right in my house!"

Owl was flying over the Hundred-Acre Wood. Down below, he noticed Eeyore in the thistle patch. And next to the old gray donkey, something was gleaming.

"Hello, Eeyore!" Owl shouted down.

"Thanks for noticing me, Owl," said Eeyore.

Owl swooped down to the ground. There, among the purple thistles, were two battered tin pots.

"This is a rare and ancient treasure, probably from long ago," said Owl, proudly shining up one of the pots. "And everyone who visits my house will admire it!"

Eeyore also shined up *his* pot.
  "So that's what I look like," he said, seeing his reflection in the pot.
"This is just what I needed—a mirror. Now I can make sure that my
tail is still attached."

Piglet was outside sweeping when he discovered one of the tin pots near his house.

"I have so much cleaning to do today," said Piglet, filling the pot with soapsuds. "This will really be a big help."

And he happily began to scrub.

Tigger and Roo went back to Kanga's house and told her that the five pots had disappeared.

"It's a mystery, Mama!" Roo told Kanga.

"Yep. Those pots must have just flown away," added Tigger.
"Or bounced away," said Kanga. "Now you two must go back and
look for them. We don't want to litter the Hundred-Acre Wood."

"You look down. I'll look up," Tigger told Roo as they retraced their steps back through the forest.

"Do you see any pots, Tigger?" asked Roo.

"Nope. Just Eeyore looking in a mirror," answered Tigger. "No pots at all."

As Tigger and Roo passed by Owl's house, Owl called down to them. "Would you like to come up and see my rare and ancient treasure?"

"Gee, we'd love to, Owl, but right now we're looking for a bunch of old pots we lost," said Tigger.

"Oh," replied Owl, disappointed. "Well, if you ever want to see a rare and ancient treasure, please feel free to call on me."

"Maybe Rabbit found the pots," Tigger suggested as he knocked on Rabbit's door.

But all Rabbit wanted to talk about was his new planter.

"That's tiggerific, Long Ears, but we're looking for a bunch of old pots," Tigger told Rabbit.

"Well, there are no old pots here," Rabbit replied.

Piglet was busy scrubbing when Tigger and Roo arrived.

"Sorry for the mess," said Piglet.

"That's okay," said Tigger. "We're looking for a bunch of old pots."

"I don't have any *old* pots. But I do have a *new* pot. Would you like to borrow it?" asked Piglet.

Tigger and Roo said, "No, thanksaroo" and left.

Next, Tigger and Roo came across Pooh, who was sitting sadly on a tree stump.

"What's the matter, Pooh?" asked Roo.

"Oh, bother," said Pooh. "I found this pot outside my house and I filled it with honey, but now it's empty again."

Tigger turned to Roo. "Isn't it curious that on the same day we *lost* Kanga's pots, Pooh *found* a pot?"

"Yes!" said Roo, bouncing up and down. "And Piglet has a new pot and Rabbit has a new planter and Owl has a new treasure and Eeyore has a new mirror!"

"That's it!" Tigger said. "The mystery is solved! We lost Kanga's pots and our friends have found them!" Tigger bounced circles around Roo.

"I wish *I* had thought of using my old pots for those things!" said Kanga when the friends all gathered to tell her what had happened.

"Well, *theirs* may be old pots, but *I* found a rare and ancient treasure," said Owl.

"Of course," said Kanga. "And in the future, before we get rid of something, let's see if we can find another use for it—or give it to someone else who can."

Just at that moment, Pooh's tummy rumbled.

"Kanga, you wouldn't want to get rid of some cookies, would you?" he asked.

Kanga laughed. It just so happened she *did* want to get rid of some cookies, so she gave them to some friends who could use them.

And the cookies disappeared almost as fast as the pots had!